CONRAD THE SPIDER

ISBN: 9781913637149

Edit & layout Shaun Russell

Published by
Jelly Bean Books
Mackintosh House
136 Newport Road, Cardiff, CF24 1DJ
www.candyjarbooks.co.uk

IN ASSOCIATION WITH

music
children
.org

CONRAD THE SPIDER

Molly Arbuthnott

illustrated by Maude Smith

Conrad was a spider, but not an ordinary spider,
he was the top rock star spider in all the land.

The secret to his success? His legs... His eight skinny, hairy legs. Six of these he would unscrew to use as his guitar strings. They created the most unique twang, and everyone loved it!

One day, after another sell-out performance, he put his guitar down on a chair at the side of the stage and went off to sign some autographs.

When he came back his guitar was gone.
He searched high and low but there was no
sign of it anywhere...

MISSING GUITAR

Conrad wrote posters, appeared on the news and in newspapers. There was a full-on national search for his guitar, but no one could find it.

CONRAD'S GUITA

Without his guitar, no one was interested in Conrad's music anymore. And with only two legs Conrad couldn't move around very much so he got quite sad and lonely, poor old Conrad.

With no money for rent he was homeless and took to aimlessly hobbling down lonely street after lonely street.

No one was his friend anymore, no one except a poor ladybird who let Conrad share her crisp packet home by the river.

One day, Conrad was hobbling home and saw something washed up by the side of the river, it looked familiar... He rubbed his eye covers. He couldn't believe it!

There, by the side of the river, was his guitar!
The wood was a bit mauled, but all his legs were there
which was the important bit.

GUITARS

He was so happy! He quickly screwed on his legs again and took what was left of his guitar to the guitar shop for a bit of TLC.

Conrad was back and everyone loved him even more than before. And Conrad? He married his ladybird and lived happily ever after!

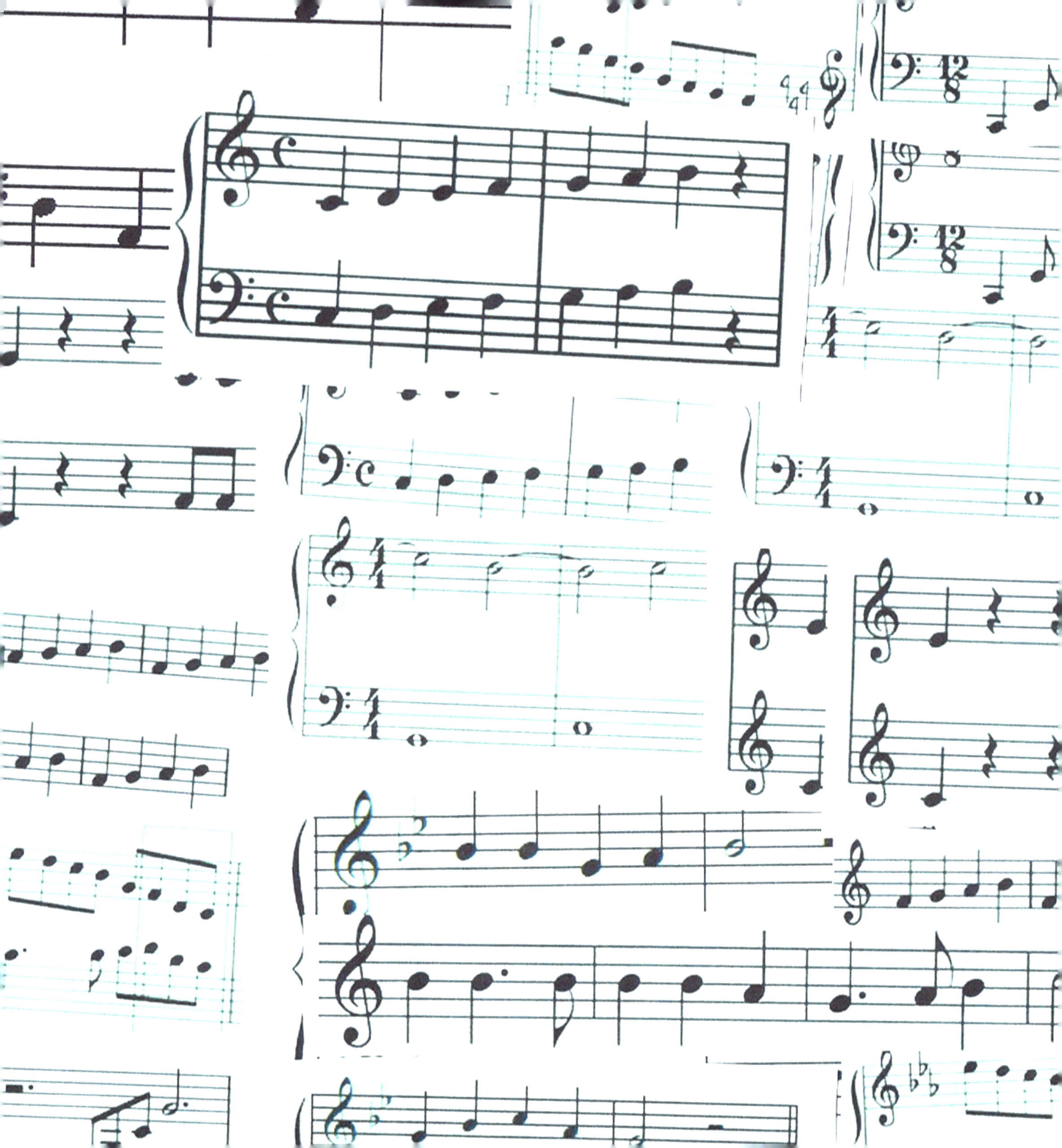

www.ingramcontent.com/pod-product-compliance
Lightning Source LLC
Chambersburg PA
CBHW040916100426
42737CB00042B/101